Para Fernando.
– *Luciano Lozano*

"BEA BAILA"
1ª edición: noviembre de 2017

Textos e ilustraciones ©Luciano Lozano
Publicado por ©Tres Tigres Tristes
Tres Tigres Tristes es un sello de Publicaciones Ilustradas TTT S.L.

Dirección editorial: Guillermo Pérez Aguilar ❤ Bárbara Centorbi Rojo
ISBN: 978-84-947304-3-6 / Depósito Legal: SE 1947-2017
Impreso en España.

 www.trestigrestristes.com

Esta obra ha recibido una ayuda a la edición del Ministerio de Educación, Cultura y Deporte.

Bea
baila

-Luciano Lozano-

Tres Tigres Tristes

—¡Buenos días! La semana que viene hay un examen de matemáticas —saludó la profesora un lunes por la mañana, cuando los niños entraban en clase.

A Bea no le gustaba estudiar. Pero sobre todo, no le gustaban nada las matemáticas.

Se aburría en el colegio,
y nunca sacaba buenas notas.

Un día,
su madre recibió una terrible,
terrible carta del colegio. Decía que Bea no
pasaría de curso si no lograba aprenderse las
tablas de multiplicar.

Así que decidió contratar a un profesor
particular.

Pero Bea no era capaz de concentrarse.

«¿Qué le estará pasando a Bea?»,
se preguntó su mamá. Y la llevó a ver a su doctora
que, viendo que todo estaba en su sitio, le recomendó
visitar un psicólogo.

Bea creía que no tenía ningún problema,
pero todo el mundo estaba empeñado en pensar lo contrario.

Se sentía confundida y triste.

Bea y su madre fueron a ver al psicólogo,
dispuestas a encontrar una solución definitiva.

Tras observarla y escucharla,
el psicólogo se acercó a Bea y le dijo:

—Voy a salir un momento con tu
madre. Espéranos aquí.

Pero antes de salir, el psicólogo
encendió la radio, y dejó la habitación
envuelta en una suave melodía.

Por un momento, Bea olvidó dónde
estaba. Sonrió y cerró los ojos mientras
su cuerpo se movía con gracia al ritmo
de la música.

La madre de Bea nunca había visto a su hija moverse así antes. El psicólogo carraspeó un poco, y anunció con una voz grave:

—¡Señora, su hija no está enferma! ¡Su hija es una bailarina!

«¿Soy una bailarina?
                    ¡Soy una bailarina!», pensó Bea.

—¡Le recomiendo que lleve a su hija a una escuela de danza! — sentenció finalmente el psicólogo.

En la escuela de danza había muchas niñas y niños que no paraban de moverse. Justo como ella.

Cuando su mamá se marchó, Bea se puso a bailar con todos los demás niños.

Bea sentía que flotaba sobre el suelo. Todos sonreían y no necesitaban hablar.
Se sintió feliz.

Bea se pasaba toda la semana esperando
a que llegara el miércoles por la tarde
para ir a clase de danza.

Practicaba todos los días en su casa mientras
recitaba la tabla de multiplicar.

Bea descubrió que le resultaba más fácil pensar
y estar atenta mientras se movía.

Ahora
se lo pasaba bien incluso en el colegio.

—¡Veintisiete! —gritó Bea cuando
la profesora preguntó cuánto eran
tres por nueve.

Por las noches, soñaba que bailaba y repetía sus pasos de baile favoritos.

Puede que Bea llegase a bailar en un gran teatro algún día.

Puede que no.

Instead of gathering berries the next day, Boo gazed thoughtfully across the meadow.

"Peekaboo!" Talena jumped from behind a bush. "I have been looking for you! Come, I will show you where I found a luscious blackberry patch."

"Thank you, Talena," said Boo, "but I'm not very hungry today."

"It's not like you to turn down blackberries! Is there something wrong, Boo?"

"Since I heard the stories Frances told, I can think of nothing else," Boo said. "I want to go and see for myself, Talena."

"Where, Boo? Go where?"

"Past the meadow, beyond the owl's nest, to a place where the sun rests at night."

Talena was very quiet. "But Boo," she said slowly, "no Peek-A-Boo bear has ever left our forest."

Boo sighed. Perhaps Talena was right.

But even though he tried very hard to be happy in his forest home, at night Boo's dreams carried him far, far away.

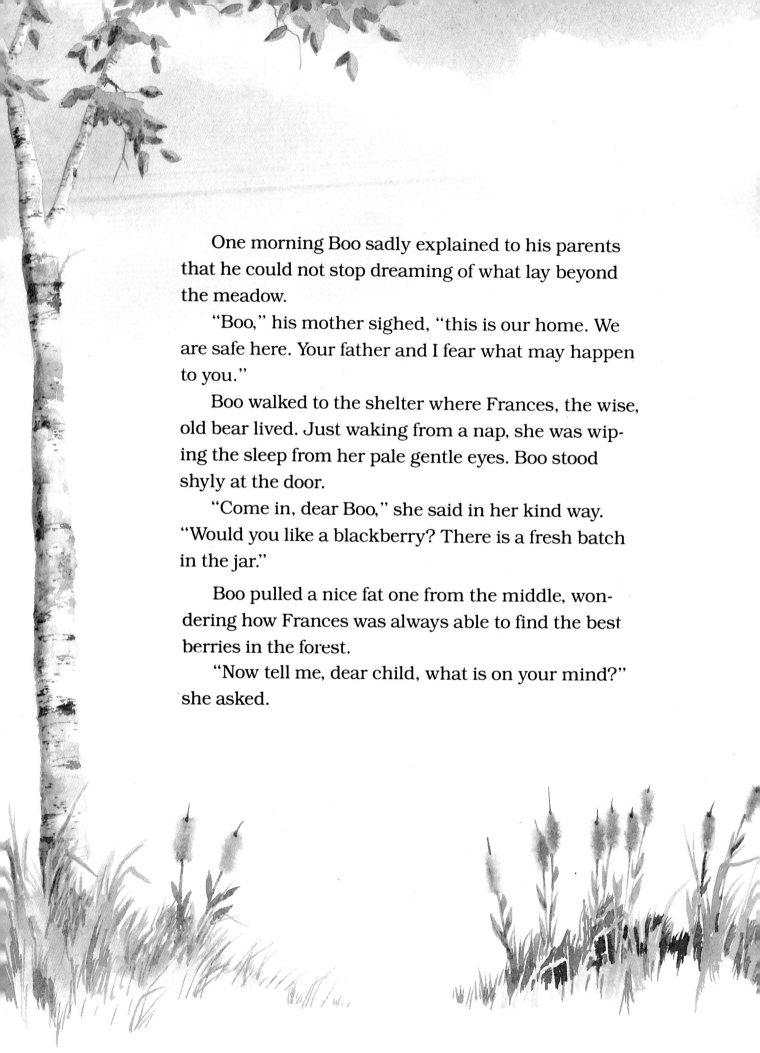

One morning Boo sadly explained to his parents that he could not stop dreaming of what lay beyond the meadow.

"Boo," his mother sighed, "this is our home. We are safe here. Your father and I fear what may happen to you."

Boo walked to the shelter where Frances, the wise, old bear lived. Just waking from a nap, she was wiping the sleep from her pale gentle eyes. Boo stood shyly at the door.

"Come in, dear Boo," she said in her kind way. "Would you like a blackberry? There is a fresh batch in the jar."

Boo pulled a nice fat one from the middle, wondering how Frances was always able to find the best berries in the forest.

"Now tell me, dear child, what is on your mind?" she asked.

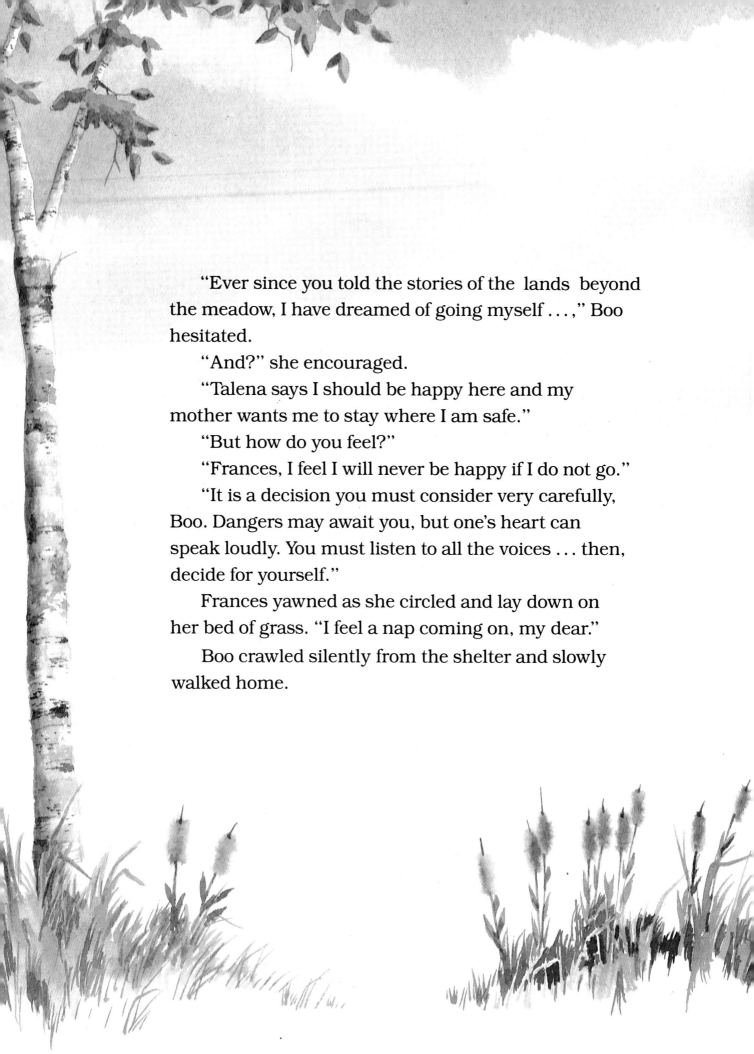

"Ever since you told the stories of the lands beyond the meadow, I have dreamed of going myself . . . ," Boo hesitated.

"And?" she encouraged.

"Talena says I should be happy here and my mother wants me to stay where I am safe."

"But how do you feel?"

"Frances, I feel I will never be happy if I do not go."

"It is a decision you must consider very carefully, Boo. Dangers may await you, but one's heart can speak loudly. You must listen to all the voices . . . then, decide for yourself."

Frances yawned as she circled and lay down on her bed of grass. "I feel a nap coming on, my dear."

Boo crawled silently from the shelter and slowly walked home.

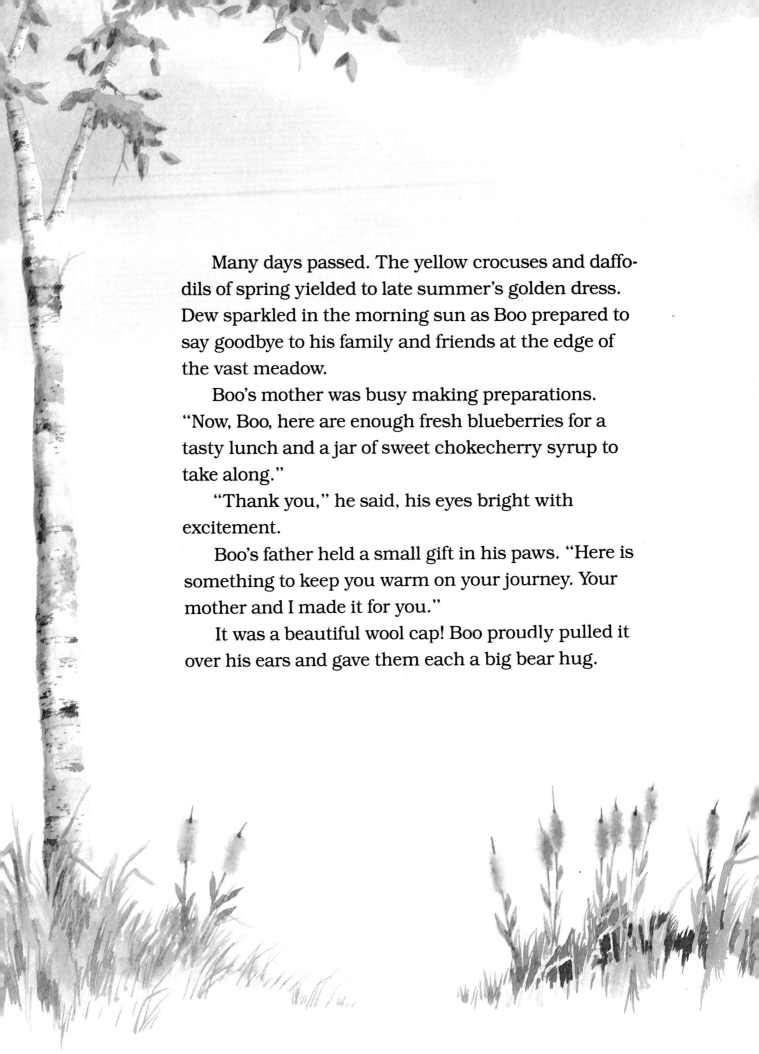

Many days passed. The yellow crocuses and daffo-
dils of spring yielded to late summer's golden dress.
Dew sparkled in the morning sun as Boo prepared to
say goodbye to his family and friends at the edge of
the vast meadow.

Boo's mother was busy making preparations.
"Now, Boo, here are enough fresh blueberries for a
tasty lunch and a jar of sweet chokecherry syrup to
take along."

"Thank you," he said, his eyes bright with
excitement.

Boo's father held a small gift in his paws. "Here is
something to keep you warm on your journey. Your
mother and I made it for you."

It was a beautiful wool cap! Boo proudly pulled it
over his ears and gave them each a big bear hug.

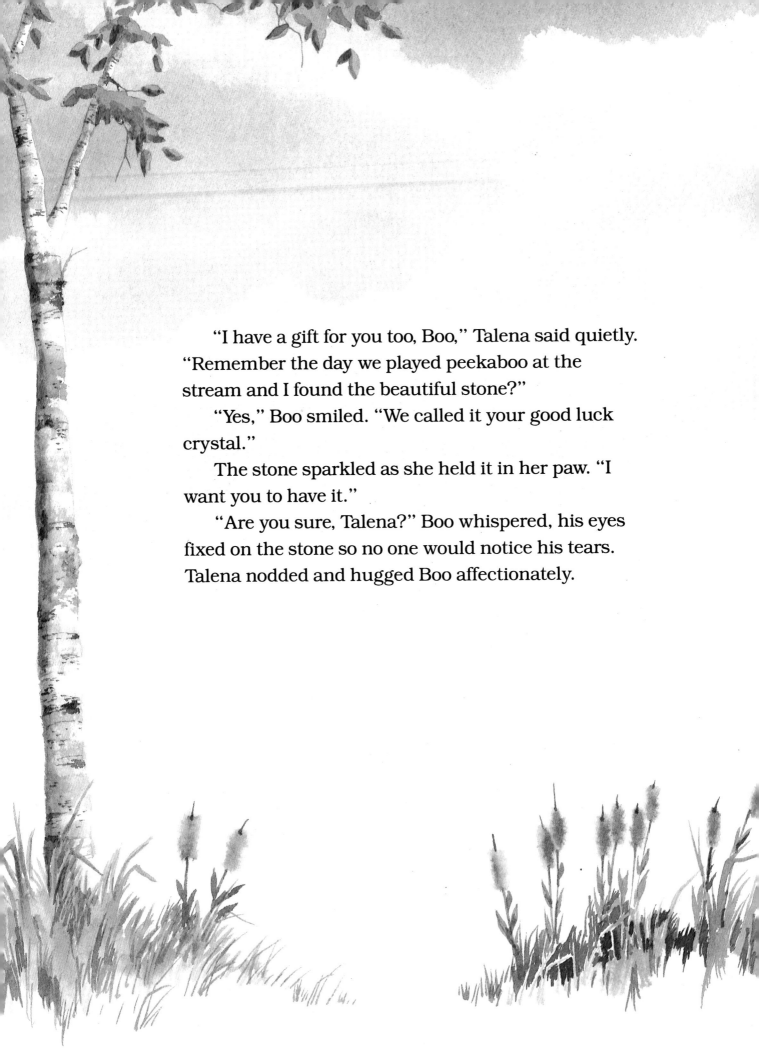

"I have a gift for you too, Boo," Talena said quietly. "Remember the day we played peekaboo at the stream and I found the beautiful stone?"

"Yes," Boo smiled. "We called it your good luck crystal."

The stone sparkled as she held it in her paw. "I want you to have it."

"Are you sure, Talena?" Boo whispered, his eyes fixed on the stone so no one would notice his tears. Talena nodded and hugged Boo affectionately.

Ambling towards the meadow, Frances caught Boo's eye. "So, the big day has finally arrived," she said. "Are you ready for your great adventure?"

Boo laughed and said he felt like dancing. "But a part of me also yearns to be home in my soft bed. Is it strange that I should feel both, Frances?" he asked.

"Not at all, my dear Boo," she answered. "Few things in life are as clear as Talena's crystal!"

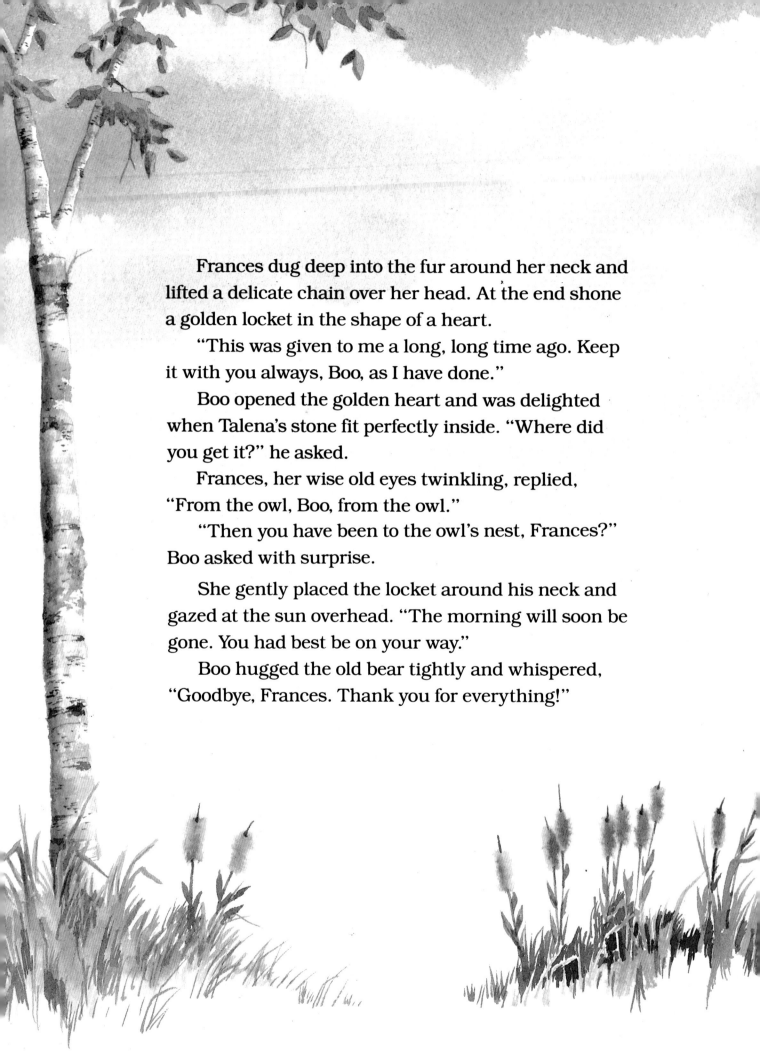

Frances dug deep into the fur around her neck and lifted a delicate chain over her head. At the end shone a golden locket in the shape of a heart.

"This was given to me a long, long time ago. Keep it with you always, Boo, as I have done."

Boo opened the golden heart and was delighted when Talena's stone fit perfectly inside. "Where did you get it?" he asked.

Frances, her wise old eyes twinkling, replied, "From the owl, Boo, from the owl."

"Then you have been to the owl's nest, Frances?" Boo asked with surprise.

She gently placed the locket around his neck and gazed at the sun overhead. "The morning will soon be gone. You had best be on your way."

Boo hugged the old bear tightly and whispered, "Goodbye, Frances. Thank you for everything!"

The journey had finally begun. Boo could hear Talena and his mother and father calling out above all the others, "Farewell, Boo! Good Luck! We love you!"

"Farewell, Boo! Good Luck! We love you!"

Boo clutched the locket tightly in his paw and turned once more to wave goodbye. As the owl flew high above the meadow, Boo bravely marched toward the many adventures that lay ahead.

In the stories to follow, Boo discovers the true value of the gifts from home as he ventures far beyond the owl's nest. The golden heart gives strength and courage and Talena's crystal brings understanding. The wool cap reminds Boo of the loving Peek-A-Boo bears in the meadow and warms his heart.